Polka-dot
Fixes Kindergarten

Catherine Urdahl

Illustrated by Mai S. Kemble

ini Charlesbridge

With much love to Dad, who really can fix anything—C. U.

For my family, who all helped me feel at home. And Josh, for believing in me—M. S. K.

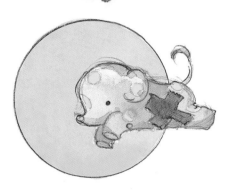

Text copyright © 2011 by Catherine Nelson-Urdahl
Illustrations copyright © 2011 by Mai S. Kemble

Published by Charlesbridge
85 Main Street
Watertown, MA 02472
(617) 926-0329
www.charlesbridge.com

Library of Congress Cataloging-in-Publication Data
Urdahl, Catherine.
    Polka-dot fixes kindergarten / Catherine Urdahl ; illustrated by Mai Kemble.
        p. cm.
    Summary: On the first day of kindergarten, Polka-dot uses the fix-it kit her grandpa
has prepared for her to help her make a friend.
    ISBN 978-1-57091-737-0 (reinforced for library use)
    ISBN 978-1-57091-738-7 (softcover)
[1. First day of school—Fiction. 2. Kindergarten—Fiction. 3.Schools—Fiction.
4. Repairing—Fiction.] I. Kemble, Mai S., ill. II. Title.
PZ7.U638Po 2011
[E]—dc22   2010023530

Printed in Singapore
(hc) 10 9 8 7 6 5 4 3 2 1
(sc) 10 9 8 7 6 5 4 3 2 1

Illustrations done in watercolor, Prismacolor colored pencils, and graphite
    on 300-lb. Arches hot-press paper
Display type and text type set in Blue Century and Sabon
Color separations by Chroma Graphics, Singapore
Printed and bound February 2011 by Imago in Singapore
Production supervision by Brian G. Walker
Designed by Martha MacLeod Sikkema

For Polka-dot's whole life, Grandpa had fixed everything.

When she tore her favorite dress,
Grandpa mended it lickety-split with
duct tape.

When she smeared her
ladybug tattoo, he scrubbed it
off with runny soap.

When she fell into the prickly bushes,
he covered her legs with
dotted bandages.

Grandpa had fixed everything, but starting today
Polka-dot was on her own. Today she was a kindergartner.
"Are you ready?" asked Grandpa.
Polka-dot peered into her fix-it kit: duct tape,
runny soap, dotted bandages. It was just like Grandpa's.

Polka-dot zipped her kit and stuffed it in her pocket.

Now she was ready for anything.

When they reached kindergarten, Grandpa gave
Polka-dot a good-bye squeeze. "Keep that kit handy."

The teacher shook Polka-dot's hand. "I'm Mrs. Jackson."

A girl with a striped dress tugged at Mrs. Jackson's elbow.

"Just a minute, please," said Mrs. Jackson.

The girl's shoulders slumped. Then, fast as a flash, she stuck out her tongue—right at Polka-dot.

Polka-dot pretended not to notice.

Mrs. Jackson pinned a name tag to Polka-dot's sweater. It said *Dorothy*.

Polka-dot scrunched her nose. "That was my baby name. I'm Polka-dot now."

"Oops," said Mrs. Jackson. "We can fix that later."

Polka-dot jiggled her fix-it kit.
Grandpa would have fixed it
right away.

Before Mrs. Jackson turned to the next kindergartner,
Polka-dot handed her a bouquet of dotted pencils.
Mrs. Jackson smiled so big Polka-dot could see a gold tooth.

The striped-dress girl gasped out loud. Then she whispered in Polka-dot's ear. "I was going to bring her pencils. You're a copycat."

Polka-dot felt her cheeks turn pink. She looked away so the girl wouldn't see.

Mrs. Jackson called everyone to sit in a circle. "I've taught kindergarten for years and years," she said. "I'm as old as the moon."

Soon it was Polka-dot's turn to talk. "My name is Polka-dot, and I like dots and spots."

The striped-dress girl waved her hand. "I like stripes. My mom says they make me look grown-up."

"Please wait your turn, Liz," said Mrs. Jackson. "That's a kindergarten rule."

Liz glared at Polka-dot. "Polka dots are for babies," she whispered.

Stripes are for meanies, thought Polka-dot.

"Time for art," said Mrs. Jackson after everyone had a turn to talk. Polka-dot sat up straight. She loved to paint. *Swish, swish.* She painted blue clouds across the paper. "Blue is a boy color," said Liz.

"I'm not finished." Polka-dot jammed the brush into
the red paint.

"Blue brush in the blue cup. That's a kindergarten rule."
Mrs. Jackson's lips made a skinny smile. "We don't want
to spoil the paint."

Polka-dot yanked the brush out of the cup. *Oh, no, no, no.* The brush was dripping purple on the floor.

Polka-dot felt her face turn red-hot. *What would Grandpa do?* Speedy-quick, she reached into her fix-it kit and poured runny soap on the spot.

The spot just grew.

"You are SO messy," said Liz in a really loud voice.

Mrs. Jackson looked straight at Polka-dot and Liz. "Unless we have something nice to say, we don't say anything at all. That's a kindergarten rule."

"My mom says it's *good* to tell the truth," Liz whispered in a shaky voice. "And you *did* make a mess."

Polka-dot covered the purple blotch with her foot. She would not use the paint again—not ever.

"Time for recess," said Mrs. Jackson.

At recess Polka-dot stared through the fence. She could not wait to see Grandpa. She would tell him kindergarten was bad, BAD, **BAD!** She would tell him the kids were mean. And the teacher just cared about her paint.

Polka-dot reached into her fix-it kit. She stuck six dotted bandages on all different spots, but she didn't feel one bit better.

She couldn't fix anything.

Slap, slap, slap. It was Liz jumping rope.
"Polka, Polka, Polka-dot.
Wears a dress that's for a tot."

Polka-dot squeezed her eyes shut. *Do not cry, do not cry.*

Sneaking a hand into her pocket, she rubbed her fix-it kit. A piece of duct tape could stop Liz's mean mouth, but Mrs. Jackson probably had rules about duct tape.

Polka-dot took a tiny step toward Liz. "Your mouth is mean, mean, mean. Every time it opens, more mean words pop out."

Liz stepped back, smack into the fence.

"Look what you made me do! I'm stuck!"

Liz gave her dress a yank.

Rip!

"I see London, I see France . . . ," said one of the boys.
Uh-oh, thought Polka-dot. *He's going to say "underpants."*

"Don't say it!" cried Liz. She tried to cover the rip.

Polka-dot looked at Liz's watery eyes, and the anger leaked right out of her.

This time she knew for sure what to do. She took a
deep breath. "I can fix that."

While Liz squeezed the rip together, Polka-dot stuck
on the duct tape.

Liz rubbed her toe in the dirt. "Thanks," she finally said.

"You're welcome," said Polka-dot.

Liz glanced up. "Your name tag is wrong."

"Mrs. Jackson said we'd fix it later," said Polka-dot.

Liz stared through the fence. "If my mom were here,
she'd fix it now."

Polka-dot sighed. "So would my grandpa."

The bell rang, and the class marched inside.

Liz pulled Polka-dot to the art corner. "I have an idea."
Liz cut out dots, and Polka-dot squeezed on glue.
Together they made the fanciest name tag ever.

Mrs. Jackson smiled extra-wide at Polka-dot and Liz.
She handed Polka-dot a dotted pencil. "This time, I'll let
you write it yourself."

After kindergarten Grandpa was waiting at the door.

"This is Liz," said Polka-dot.

Grandpa shook Liz's hand. "Stripes—snazzy."

"Dots are okay, too," said Liz. "See you tomorrow!"

Grandpa nodded at Polka-dot. "Nice job with the duct tape."

Squeezing her fix-it kit, Polka-dot stood tall. "Now I can fix almost anything."